THE LITTLE PRINCE

Antoine de Saint-Exupéry

The Little Prince

Translated by Ros and Chloe Schwartz

With an introduction by Kate Mosse

PICADOR CLASSIC

This Picador Classic edition first published 2015 by Picador
an imprint of Pan Macmillan
20 New Wharf Road, London N1 9RR
Associated companies throughout the world
www.panmacmillan.com

ISBN 978-1-5098-1130-4

Originally published in 1943 as *Le Petit Prince* by Reynal & Hitchcock, New York

1 3 5 7 9 8 6 4 2

A CIP catalogue record for this book is available from the British Library.

Printed and bound by CPI Group (UK) Ltd, Croydon, CR0 4YY

Visit **www.picador.com/classic** to read more about all our books
and to buy them. You will also find features, author interviews and
news of any author events, and you can sign up for e-newsletters
so that you're always first to hear about our new releases.

Introduction

'Il était une fois un petit prince qui habitait
une planète à peine plus grande que lui,
et qui avait besoin d'un ami.'

'Once upon a time there was a little prince who lived
on a planet not much bigger than himself and
was in need of a friend.'

The narrator of *Le Petit Prince* – an aviator whose plane has
crashed in the desert – says he wishes he could start his story in
this way. Write a fairytale. Instead, he begins with a story about
himself as a six-year-old child. About how the reaction of adults
to something he'd drawn put him off drawing. About how he
realized, then, that grown-ups were incapable of seeing what
mattered. Rather than a boa constrictor eating an elephant,
all they could see was a dull, everyday kind of a hat. It is the
first example of what will be one of the book's refrains: that
'les grandes personnes sont décidément bien bizarres.' 'Grown-ups
really are very strange.'

The tone is set. But if it's not a fairytale, then what is it?
A parable, if one defines a parable as a simple, didactic tale illus-
trating some deeper moral or spiritual lesson? Or, better perhaps,
a fable. A fable has many of the same characteristics, except there
are animals, plants and inanimate objects alongside people.

What about allegory? Where everything is intended to stand for, to illuminate, something else.

These literary definitions, if they matter at all, blur one into the other and the purpose, style and nature of these kinds of layered works – from Paulo Coelho's *The Alchemist* (1993), Kipling's *Just So Stories* (1902), John Bunyan's *The Pilgrim's Progress* (1678) to going right back to the New Testament or Aesop's Fables (620–560 BCE) – vary. Some were written for adults, some expressly for children, some for both. What matters is the intention that one's interpretation of what lies beneath the surface is as important – more so – than what lies on the page. The longevity of these stories rests in their power to speak beyond their own era, beyond the time and context within which they were written, to state universal truths.

Le Petit Prince, first published in 1943 in English and French in the US (only in 1945 in Antoine de Saint-Exupéry's native France) is such a book. A philosophical, lyrical children's story beloved of adults. To date, it has sold some 140 million copies worldwide – and continues to sell roughly two million new copies each year. It's been translated into 250 languages, is said to be the third most translated book in the world and, in France, was voted Best Book of the 20th Century. It has inspired radio and television plays, stage plays and feature films, ballets, verse adaptations, paintings and sculptures.

And yet . . . I never particularly enjoyed fables or children's books adopted – claimed – by adults. I preferred a writer to come out and say what they meant, rather than wrapping it up in a riddle. And I noticed that, in so many of these parables or allegories intended to reveal insights into some shared, universal human experience, there were few female characters. Girls rarely got a look in.

So, for years, I avoided *Le Petit Prince*. Wrongly. And although I could see that the observations about childhood were terrific – and agreed that grown-ups really often are '*bien bizarres*' – I didn't think there was anything in the book for me.

Little by little, though, I began to change my mind. Ten years ago, on a wall in the medieval city of Carcassonne in southwest France – where most of my historical fiction is set – I noticed a street sign. Rue de Antoine Saint-Exupéry. It was a rather modest road, in a shabby part of town, and I stopped, wondering why he was honoured in Languedoc. I discovered that de Saint-Exupéry had worked in Toulouse in the 1920s for Aéropostale. It seemed a slight link and reading is so often a matter of stumbling upon the right book at the right time. The stories that stay with us, which we return to time and again throughout our lives, are often rooted in a personal affection, the ways in which a particular tale speaks to us. So although I had another go – the tale of a little prince in a golden scarf, who shares the story of how he has come to Earth from his own planet, visiting six other planets en route – didn't grab me. I thought it charming, but it wasn't to my taste. Besides, I was writing and my head was full of medieval history and heresy.

Another summer passed. Another. Then a couple of years ago, the French daily newspaper *Le Monde* published a survey about the most frequently used names for schools, colleges, academies: Antoine de Saint-Exupéry was there at No. 8 in the list. What's more, he was one of the few authors celebrated both by his name (418 schools) and for his work (there are 98 institutions called *Le Petit Prince*.) The airport in Lyon, I learnt, was named after him.

This time, I did a little biographical research. Antoine Marie Jean-Baptiste Roger, comte de Saint Exupéry, was born in Lyon on 29 June 1900 into a wealthy aristocratic family. The third of five children (three sisters and a younger brother), his father died when he was four, radically changing the family's circumstances. His brother François was to die of rheumatic fever at the age of fifteen. Antoine later wrote of his death of how François 'remained motionless for an instant. He did not cry out. He fell as gently as a [young] tree falls'. This description echoes very closely the lyrical ending of *Le Petit Prince*.

After twice failing his exams at a preparatory Naval Academy, he enrolled at the École des Beaux-Arts to study architecture. Again, he did not graduate. Instead, he drifted in and out of occupations, before beginning his military service in 1921. There, he took flying lessons, and the seeds were sown. He transferred from the Army to the French Air Force, then worked for the fledgling air postal service flying between Toulouse and Dakar. He published his first novella, *L'Aviateur*, followed in 1929 by a full-length work, *Courrier Sud* (*Southern Mail*). His dual career as a writer and aviator had begun. His reputation was confirmed in 1931 with the publication of *Vol de Nuit* (*Night*

Flight), which won the prestigious Prix Femina. That same year, he married the Salvadoran writer and artist Consuelo Suncín. It was to be a stormy on-off marriage.

I read on. He went on to win the Grand Prix du Roman de l'Académie Française, a US National Book Award in 1939 for *Terres des Hommes* (*Wind, Sand and Stars*), a lyrical biographical work which was in part inspired by his near-fatal crash in the Sahara Desert in 1935. He was awarded a Croix de Guerre in 1940, then posthumously both the inaugural Prix des Ambassadeurs and a Croix de Guerre avec Palme. At the outbreak of the Second World War in 1939, de Saint-Exupéry re-joined the French Air Force, flying reconnaissance missions until the Armistice with Germany. After an unhappy period of writing exile in America, he returned to Europe and joined the Free French forces. Then, I came to the final heart-stopping line of biography. On 31 July 1944, on a mission to collect information on Nazi troop movements in the Rhone Valley, de Saint-Exupéry had vanished off the coast of Marseille. Missing, presumed dead.

As a rule, I dislike the tendency to interpret a writer's work through the prism of their real lives. Fiction is imagination not autobiography. Novels should be allowed to stand for themselves, speak for themselves. At the same time, it was obvious de Saint-Exupéry's life was significantly present in his writings. And I understood too, now, why he was a French national hero. Excelling in different disciplines, yet a man often out of step with the world. He was celebrated and successful, with friends and lovers, yet often lonely and unhappy. Out of these contradictions had come *Le Petit Prince*. Like several other children's authors – Louisa May Alcott, for example – Saint-Exupéry wrote (and illustrated) the book on the advice of a friend. And he wrote, in some ways, for himself. To try to make sense of his sadness and alienation.

By now, I was researching and writing the third of my Languedoc Trilogy, *Citadel*, which is set during the Occupation of Carcassonne between June 1942 and August 1944. Again, I was tramping the street of the Bastide in the heat of the afternoon, mapping the stories of my imagined characters. Jotting down the names of the Carcassonnais Resistance executed in August 1944 commemorated on road signs and war memorials. Walking down the Allée d'Iéna, hearing in my imagination the rumble of Wehrmacht tanks, I found myself back at the Rue de Saint-Exupéry. This time, I knew that de Saint-Exupéry also had died fighting the Nazi Occupation.

For the third time, I went back to *Le Petit Prince*. This time I didn't skim over the Dedication. He begins by dedicating the book to Léon Werth. Werth, a close friend of 'Tonio', was a French Jewish writer, active in the Resistance, an erudite and highly respected social historian who survived the war. De Saint-Exupéry then apologizes and explains why he has dedicated the book to a grown-up: Werth is his best friend; Werth understands everything (even children's books); that Werth lives in France 'where he is hungry and cold and needs comforting'. He amends the dedication: '*A Léon Werth quand il était petit garçon*'. For Léon Werth, the little boy that was.

That was it. The story of the story, the blurring of biography and inspiration, the understanding that de Saint-Exupéry was talking as much to his young self – and the lost child in all of us – as well as to his young readers, I was hooked. Finally, I fell in love with *Le Petit Prince*.

It is a gem of a book, a beautiful and elegiac philosophical story of love and friendship, a reflection on how to distinguish what matters and what does not. It is a parable and a fairytale and a fable rolled into one, a story about innocence and loneliness, about stripping away the restricting and sketchy values of the adult world. A book about greed, pointless ambition, conformity, disappointment, self-importance and racism (the Turkish Astronomer, who discovers a new asteroid in 1909, is not taken seriously until he forsakes his own clothes for a Western suit and tie). A story about the singing of the stars and the glory of the setting sun.

Each reader will take her or his own lessons from *Le Petit Prince*, so here are just a few: that authority over others for no purpose is pointless, as is the accumulation of wealth for its own sake (the man who counts stars, in order to say he owns them, is unhappy); that loneliness and sadness are shared human conditions – 'not everybody has had a friend' but that it can be 'lonely among people too' – but one saves oneself by caring for others; that sometimes it doesn't matter if you put off a job until later, but sometimes – in the case of the baobabs that threaten to over-run their planet – it does.

Under-pinning everything are two things: the belief that if

we could learn to rediscover joy for no other reason than to lift our spirits, then we will be more content. And that we should learn – as the fox counsels the Little Prince – how to look beneath the surface of things to what really matters.

'Voici mon secret. Il est très simple: on ne voit bien qu'avec le cœur. L'essentiel est invisible pour les yeux.'

'This is my secret. It's very simple. You only see clearly with your heart. The most important things are invisible to the eyes.'

KATE MOSSE

JULY 2015

PS. Oh, it's true. Grown-ups really are very strange!

For Léon Werth

I apologise to children for dedicating this book to a grown-up. But I have a good excuse: this grown-up is the best friend I have ever had. I have another excuse too: this grown-up understands everything, even books for children. And I have a third excuse: this grown-up lives in France where he is hungry and cold and needs comforting. If these reasons are not enough, I should like to dedicate this book to the child this grown-up once was. All grown-ups were children once (but most of them have forgotten). So I will alter my dedication:

For Léon Werth,
the little boy that was.

One

When I was six years old, I came across a beautiful picture in a book about the jungle called *True Stories*. It showed a boa constrictor swallowing a wild animal. This is what it looked like.

In the book it said: 'Boa constrictors swallow their prey whole, without chewing it. Afterwards they are unable to move. Then they sleep for six months while they digest.'

That set me thinking about all the things that go on in the jungle and, with a crayon, I did my first drawing. I called it drawing number one. It looked like this:

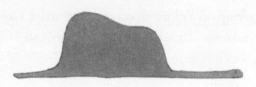

I showed my masterpiece to the grown-ups and asked if they found it scary.

They answered: 'What's scary about a hat?'

But my drawing was not of a hat. It was a boa constrictor digesting an elephant. So then I drew the inside of the boa, to help the grown-ups understand. They always need explanations. This is what my drawing number two looked like:

The grown-ups told me to forget about drawing elephants inside boa constrictors and to concentrate instead on geography, history, arithmetic and grammar. Which is why, at the age of six, seeing as my drawing number one and my drawing number two had been such a disaster, I gave up on a glorious career as an artist. Grown-ups never understand anything on their own, and it's a nuisance for children to have to keep explaining things over and over again.

So I had to choose another profession, and I learned to be a pilot. I flew all around the world. And it is true that geography came in very handy. I could tell the difference between China and Arizona at a glance. Which is very useful, if you lose your way at night.

Over the years, I have met lots of sensible people and spent a lot of time living in the world of grown-ups. I have seen them at close quarters, which has done nothing to change my opinion of them.

Whenever I met a grown-up who seemed fairly intelligent, I would test him with my drawing number one, which I have always kept, to find out if he really was perceptive. But he would always reply: 'It's a hat.' So instead of talking to him about boa constrictors or the jungle or the stars, I'd come down to his level and discuss bridge, golf, politics and neckties. And the grown-up would be delighted to meet such a reasonable man.

Two

And so I lived alone, with no one I could really talk to, until six years ago when my plane broke down in the Sahara Desert. As I did not have a mechanic with me, or any passengers, I was going to have to make a complicated engine repair on my own. My life depended on it, since I had barely enough drinking water to last a week.

The first night, I lay down on the ground and fell asleep, miles and miles from any living soul. I was more cut off than a castaway adrift in the middle of the ocean. So you can imagine my astonishment when I was awakened at daybreak by a funny little voice saying: 'Please, will you draw me a little lamb!'

'What!'

'Draw me a little lamb . . .'

I leaped to my feet as if I had been struck by lightning. I rubbed my eyes and stared. And I saw the most extraordinary little fellow studying me intently. This is the best picture I have managed to draw of him from memory.

But of course my drawing is not nearly as delightful as the original. That is not my fault; the grown-ups had put a stop to my artistic career when I was six and I had never drawn anything other than my two boa constrictors.

I gazed at him in amazement. I was miles and miles from any living soul, remember. But my little fellow did not look lost. Nor did he seem weak with exhaustion, or hunger, or thirst, or fright. In no way did he look like a child lost in the middle of the desert miles and miles from any living soul. When at last I found my voice, I said to him: 'What on earth are you doing here?'

And he repeated, very quietly, as if it were a matter of the utmost seriousness: 'Please, will you draw me a little lamb.'

Here I was, miles and miles from any living soul and with my life in danger, but I was so baffled that I meekly prepared to do as he asked and took a pen and paper out of my pocket. And then I remembered that I had mostly studied geography, history, arithmetic and grammar, and I told the little fellow (somewhat irritably) that I couldn't draw. And he replied: 'It doesn't matter. Draw me a little lamb.'

As I had never done a picture of a lamb, I presented him with one of the only two drawings I could do: a boa constrictor from the outside. And I was astounded to hear the little fellow say: 'No! No! I don't want an elephant inside a boa. A boa's too dangerous, and an elephant takes up too much room. My place is tiny. I need a lamb. Draw me a little lamb.'

So I drew.

He scrutinised my effort and said: 'No! That one looks very sickly. Draw another one.'

I drew:

My little friend smiled indulgently: 'Can't you see . . . that's not a lamb, it's a ram. It's got horns.'

So I started all over again.

But again, he turned it down: 'That one's too old. I want a lamb that will live for a long time.' I was in a hurry to start stripping down the engine and my patience was wearing thin, so I hastily sketched this:

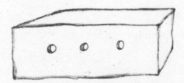

And I said: 'That's the crate. The lamb you want is inside.'

And I was amazed to see my young critic's face light up: 'That's exactly what I wanted! Do you think this lamb will need a lot of grass?'

'Why?'

'Because my place is tiny.'

'I'm sure there'll be enough. I've given you a very little lamb.'

He looked more closely at the drawing: 'Not that little . . . Oh look! He's fallen asleep.'

And that is how I made the acquaintance of the little prince.

Three

It took me ages to work out where the little prince came from. He asked me lots of questions but never seemed to hear mine. I gradually pieced his story together from odd things he said. For instance, when he first caught sight of my plane (I shan't draw it, I can't draw anything that complicated) he asked me: 'What's that thing?'

'It's not a thing. It flies. It's a plane. It's *my* plane.'

And I was proud to tell him that I was a pilot and I flew planes.

Then he exclaimed: 'What! You fell out of the sky!'

'Yes,' I replied modestly.

'Oh! That's funny.'

And the little prince gave a tinkling laugh which I found extremely annoying. I expect people to take my troubles seriously.

Then he added: 'So you came out of the sky too! What planet are you from?'

It suddenly dawned on me that he was giving me an important clue as to his mysterious appearance, and I said: 'You're from another planet, aren't you?'

But he did not reply. Still staring at my plane, his head: 'Of course, you can't have come from very far away in that thing.'

And he stood lost in thought for a while. Then, taking my lamb out of his pocket, he examined his treasure.

*

You can imagine how intrigued I was by his allusion to other planets.

So I tried to find out more: 'Where do you come from, little man? Where is "your place"? Where do you want to take my lamb?'

He pondered for a while and replied: 'The good thing about the crate is that at night it can be his house.'

'Exactly. And if you behave, I'll give you a rope to tie him up during the day. And a stake.'

The little prince was shocked: 'Tie him up? What a strange thing to do!'

'But if you don't tie him up, he'll wander all over the place and get lost.'

And my little friend burst out laughing again: 'But where would he go?'

'Anywhere. He'd follow his nose.'

Then the little prince remarked solemnly: 'It wouldn't matter, my place is so tiny!'

And he added wistfully: 'If you follow your nose you can't go very far.'

Four

A nd so I learned something else of great importance: that the place he came from was barely bigger than a house!

I should not have been that surprised. I knew very well that apart from the big planets like Earth, Jupiter, Mars and Venus, which have names, there are hundreds of others which are sometimes so small they can only just be seen through a telescope. When an astronomer discovers a new one, he gives it a number for a name. He calls it 'Asteroid 325', for example.

I have good reason to believe that the little prince's planet was Asteroid B 612. This asteroid has only been glimpsed once through a telescope, and that was by a Turkish astronomer in 1909.

He gave an impressive presentation of his discovery at an international astronomy conference. But nobody believed him because of his clothes. That is how grown-ups are.

Luckily for Asteroid B 612, a Turkish dictator made his people dress European-style, on pain of death. Wearing a very elegant suit, the astronomer gave his presentation again, in 1920. And this time everyone was convinced.

The reason I've told you all this about Asteroid B 612 and given you its number is because of grown-ups. Grown-ups love numbers. When you tell them about a new friend, they never ask you about the important things. They never say: 'What does his voice sound like? What are his favourite games? Does he collect butterflies?' They ask you: 'How old is he? How many brothers and sisters does he have? What does he weigh? How much does his father earn?' Only then do they feel they know him. If you say to grown-ups: 'I saw a beautiful pink brick house with geraniums on the window sills and doves on the roof,' they can't picture it. You have to say: 'I saw a house worth a million.' Then they marvel: 'What a lovely house!'

In the same way, if you say to them: 'The little prince really did exist. He was delightful and full of laughter and he asked for a little lamb. Only a real live person could want a lamb,' they shrug their shoulders and treat you like a child. But if you say: 'The planet he came from is Asteroid B 612,' then they take you seriously and leave you in peace. That is just how they are. You mustn't hold it against them. Children should be very patient with grown-ups.

But, of course, people who understand life are not bothered about numbers! I wish I could have begun this story like a fairy tale. I wish I could have written: 'Once upon a time there was a little prince who lived on a planet not much bigger than himself and was in need of a friend . . .' People who understand life would have found that much more natural.

I do not like people taking my book lightly. I find it very painful stirring up these memories. It is already six years since my friend disappeared with his lamb. I want to try and describe him so as not to forget him. It is sad to forget a friend. Not everybody has had a friend.

I don't want to become like those grown-ups who only care about numbers. So I bought a box of paints and some crayons. It is hard to take up drawing again at my age, when all you have ever done is two pictures of a boa constrictor digesting an elephant at the age of six! Of course I shall do my best to make my drawings as lifelike as possible. But I am not sure I will succeed. One drawing is fine, but the next is nothing like him at all. I also get his height wrong. Here the little prince is too tall. And in this one he is too small. I am also unsure about the colour of his clothes. So I do the best I can. Sometimes I get it right, and sometimes I get it wrong, but you will have to forgive me. My little friend never gave me any explanations. Perhaps he thought I was like him. But sadly, I'm not able to see lambs inside crates. Perhaps I am a bit like grown-ups. I must have grown old.

Five

E ach day I learned something new about the little
prince's planet, his departure or his journey. He let
things slip out gradually, in conversation. That was how,
on the third day, I found out about the baobab problem.

Once again, it was thanks to the lamb. Out of the
blue, the little prince asked me, as if troubled by a serious
doubt: 'It is true, isn't it, that lambs eat shrubs?'

'Yes, it's true.'

'Oh, that's a relief!'

I did not understand why he cared so much whether
lambs ate shrubs. But the little prince added: 'So that
means they also eat baobabs?'

I pointed out that baobabs are not shrubs but giant
trees as big as churches and that even if he took a whole

herd of elephants with him, they wouldn't be able to demolish even one baobab.

The idea of a herd of elephants made the little prince laugh: 'They'd have to stand on top of each other.'

'But before baobabs grow tall, they start off small.' He had become serious again.

'That's very true! But why do you want your little lamb to eat the baby baobabs?'

He replied: 'What a silly question!' as if it were obvious. And I had to rack my brains to work out the answer for myself.

The fact was that on the little prince's planet, there were good plants and bad plants, as there are everywhere, and good seeds from the good plants and bad seeds from the bad ones. But seeds are invisible. They sleep deep in the earth until one of them feels like stirring. Then it stretches and gingerly pushes up a charming, harmless little shoot towards the sun. If it is a radish or rose-bush shoot, you can leave it to grow in peace. But if it is a bad plant, you have to pull it up at once, the minute you have identified it. Now there were some fearsome seeds on the little prince's planet – and those were the baobab seeds.

The planet's soil was infested with them. If you leave it too late, you will never ever be able to get rid of a baobab tree, and it will overrun the entire planet. Its roots will eat their way down, and if the planet is very small and there are a great many baobabs, they will destroy it.

'It's something you have to do every day,' the little prince explained later. 'Once you've brushed your hair and cleaned your teeth, then you clean up your planet. You have to pull up the baobabs the moment you recognise them. They look just like rose bushes when they're very young. It's a very boring job but it's very easy.'

And he asked me to make a special effort and do a beautiful drawing to explain this to the children where I come from. 'It might come in handy if they go travelling one day,' he said.

'Sometimes it doesn't matter if you put off a job until later. But baobabs have to be pulled up immediately, otherwise there'll be a disaster. I know of a planet where a lazybones lived. He ignored three shrubs and . . .'

From the little prince's description, I did a drawing of that planet. I hate to preach, but so few people are aware of the menace of baobabs, and if someone gets lost on an asteroid, there are so many hazards, that for once I did as

I was told without arguing. I worked very hard at this particular drawing to warn my friends of the hidden danger. It was important to get the message across. Children, beware of baobabs! You may be wondering why there are no other drawings in this book as magnificent as the picture of the baobabs. The answer is very simple: I tried but I didn't succeed. But when I drew the baobabs, I was spurred on by a sense of urgency.

Six

O h, little prince, gradually I began to build up a picture of your cheerless life. For a long time, your only distraction had been the beautiful sunsets. I gleaned this new nugget of information on the morning of the fourth day, when you said: 'I love sunsets. Let's go and watch a sunset.'

'But we must wait.'

'Wait for what?'

'Wait for the sun to go down.'

At first you looked astonished and then you laughed at yourself and said: 'I keep forgetting where I am!'

Indeed he did. As we all know, when it is midday in America, the sun is setting over France. If you could whizz off to France instantly, you would see the sun go down.

Unfortunately, France is much too far away. But on your tiny little planet, all you had to do was swivel your chair a few inches and you could watch dusk fall whenever you wanted.

'One day, I watched forty-four sunsets!'

And a little later you added: 'You know, when a person is very, very sad, they like sunsets.'

'And were you very, very sad on the day you watched forty-four sunsets?'

But the little prince did not reply.

Seven

O n the fifth day, I stumbled upon another of the
little prince's secrets, again thanks to the lamb. He
suddenly came out with a question, as if he had silently
been mulling it over for a long time: 'If a lamb eats
shrubs, does it also eat flowers?'

'A lamb eats everything it comes across.'

'Even plants with thorns?'

'Yes. Even plants with thorns.'

'So what use are thorns?'

I had no idea. I was busy trying to undo a bolt in the
engine. I was very worried as I realised the damage might
be very serious, and my drinking water was running out
fast. I feared the worst.

'So what use are thorns?'

Once he had asked a question, the little prince never

let the matter drop. I was exasperated by the stubborn bolt and said the first thing that came into my head: 'Thorns have no use, it's just the plants being mean!'

'Oh!'

But after a silence he blurted out crossly: 'I don't believe you! Flowers are fragile. They're innocent. They make up for it as best they can by telling themselves that their thorns are scary.'

I did not reply.

Right then I was thinking: *If I can't undo this bolt, I'll have to take a hammer to it.*

Once again, the little prince broke in: 'And do you think that flowers . . . ?'

'No! No! I don't think anything!' I snapped. 'I have more serious matters to attend to!' He stared at me, bemused.

'Serious matters!'

He stared at me as I leaned over an object that he found very ugly, gripping my hammer, my fingers black with grease.

'You sound just like the grown-ups!'

That made me feel slightly ashamed. He added bitterly: 'You've got it all wrong, you get everything all muddled up!'

He really was very angry. He tossed his golden hair in the wind: 'I know a planet where there's a red-faced man.

He's never smelled a flower. He's never gazed at a star. He's never loved anyone. He's never done anything other than sums. And all day long, he repeats just like you: "I have serious matters to attend to! Worthwhile matters!" and that makes him puff up with pride. But he's not a man, he's a puffball!'

'A what?'

'A puffball!'

By now the little prince was pale with anger.

'Flowers have been making thorns for millions of years. For millions of years, sheep have been eating flowers despite their thorns. And isn't trying to understand why flowers go to so much trouble to make thorns that are no use a worthwhile thing to do? Isn't the war between sheep and flowers a serious matter? Isn't that serious and more important than a big, fat, red-faced man and his sums? And supposing I know of a flower that is absolutely unique, that is nowhere to be found except on my planet, and any minute that flower could accidentally be eaten up by a little lamb, isn't that important?'

He reddened then went on: 'If a person loves a flower that is the only one of its kind on all the millions and millions of stars, then gazing at the night sky is enough to make him happy. He says to himself: "My flower is out there somewhere." But if the lamb eats the flower, then suddenly it's as if all the stars had stopped shining. Isn't that important?'

He was too choked to utter another word. He burst into tears. Night had fallen. I had put down my tools.

I no longer cared about my hammer, my bolt, being thirsty or dying. There was a star, a planet, mine, Earth, and a little prince who needed comforting! I put my arm around him and cradled him, saying: 'The flower you love isn't in any danger . . . I'll draw a muzzle for your little lamb. I'll draw some protective netting for your flower. I . . .' I was at a loss for words. I felt very clumsy. I did not know how to reach out to him. The world of tears is so unfathomable.

Eight

I soon learned more about this flower. On the little prince's planet there had always been very simple flowers with a single row of petals which took up very little space and were no bother. They would appear one morning in the grass, and then fade the same evening. But this flower had sprouted one day from a seed that had blown in from who knows where, and the little prince had kept a close eye on the little shoot which was different from other shoots. It might have been a new type of baobab. But the shrub soon stopped growing and began to produce a flower. Watching the development of a huge bud, the little prince had a feeling that something miraculous was going to appear, but the flower took for ever preening herself in the sanctuary of her green room. She chose her colours with care. She dressed slowly, adjusting her petals one by one. She did not want to appear all crumpled like a poppy. She only wanted to reveal herself in the full bloom of her beauty. Oh yes! She was very vain! Her mysterious preparations lasted days and days. And then one morning, just as the sun was rising, she showed herself.

And the flower who had made such scrupulous preparations yawned and said: 'I've only just woken up . . . Forgive me . . . My hair's still a mess.'

The little prince was unable to hide his admiration: 'You're so beautiful!'

'I am, aren't I?' replied the flower softly. 'And I was born at the same time as the sun.'

The little prince rightly guessed that she was not exactly modest, but she was so lovely to behold!

'It's breakfast time, I think,' she said, adding:

'Would you kindly spare a thought for me?' And all ashamed, the little prince went off to find a watering can, filled it with cool water and poured it for the flower.

She soon began to plague him with her rather prickly vanity. For example, one day, speaking about her four thorns, she said to the little prince: 'Let the tigers come with their claws!'

'There aren't any tigers on my planet,' protested the little prince. 'And anyway, tigers don't eat grass.'

'I'm not grass,' replied the flower softly.

'I'm sorry.'

'I'm not at all afraid of tigers, but I can't stand draughts. You wouldn't have a screen, would you?'

Can't stand draughts . . . that's bad luck for a plant, thought the little prince. *This flower is a complicated creature.*

'At night, you need to put me under a glass dome. It's very cold on your planet. It's poorly equipped. Where I come from . . .'

But she stopped before she reached the end of her sentence. She had come as a seed. She could not have known anything of other worlds. Embarrassed at having been caught telling such a childish fib, she coughed a couple of times, to make the little prince feel bad: 'What about that screen?'

'I was about to get it but you were talking to me!'

Then she forced a cough again to make him sorry.

And so although he loved her and was eager to please her, the little prince soon grew wary of her. Her unkind words had wounded him and made him very unhappy.

'I shouldn't have listened to her,' he confided to me one day. 'You should never listen to flowers. You should gaze at them and smell them. Mine perfumed the air of my planet, but I wasn't able to enjoy it. Her talk of claws which so annoyed me should have made me feel sorry for her.'

And he told me: 'I got it all wrong! I should have judged her by her actions, not her words. She filled my life with fragrance and light. I should never have run away! I should have realised that deep down she cared, despite her ridiculous tricks. Flowers are so contrary! But I was too young to know how to love her.'

Nine

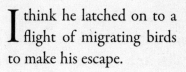

I think he latched on to a flight of migrating birds to make his escape.

On the morning of his departure, he put his planet in good order. He carefully chimney-swept the active volcanoes. There were two active volcanoes which were very useful for cooking breakfast in the morning. There was also one extinct volcano, but, as he used to say, 'You never know!' and so he chimney-swept the extinct volcano too.

If volcanoes are properly swept, they burn slowly and steadily, without erupting. Volcanic eruptions are like chimney fires. Of course, here on Earth, we are not tall enough to chimney-sweep our volcanoes. That is why they give us so much trouble.

Feeling slightly wistful, the little prince also pulled up the last baobab shoots. He thought he would never return. But that morning, he found all those familiar chores very enjoyable. And when he watered the flower for the last time and was about to put her under her protective dome, he found himself on the verge of tears.

'Goodbye,' he said to the flower.

But she did not reply.

'Goodbye,' he repeated.

The flower coughed. But it was not because of her cold.

'I've been stupid,' she said at last. 'Please forgive me. Try to be happy.'

He was surprised that she was not complaining. He stood there holding the dome, completely confused. He could not understand her calm gentleness.

'Yes, I love you,' said the flower. 'You had no idea, and that was my fault. Never mind. But you've been as stupid as me. Try to be happy. Leave that dome where it is, I don't want it any more.'

'What about the wind . . . ?'

'My cold isn't that bad. The cool night air will do me good. I am a flower.'

'What about the animals . . . ?'

'I'm going to have to cope with a few caterpillars if I want to see butterflies. I've heard they're so beautiful. Otherwise, who'll visit me? You'll be far away. As for big beasts, I'm not scared. I've got my claws.'

And she innocently bared her four thorns. Then she added: 'Stop hanging around, you're getting on my nerves. You've made up your mind, so go.'

For she didn't want him to see her cry. She was such a proud flower.

He carefully chimney-swept the active volcanoes.

Ten

The little prince found himself in the region of asteroids 325, 326, 327, 328, 329 and 330. He began by visiting them in search of something to do and to educate himself.

The first asteroid was home to a king. Robed in purple and ermine, he sat on a very simple yet majestic throne.

'Ah! Here comes a subject!' cried the king when he spotted the little prince.

And the little prince wondered: 'How does he know who I am since he's never set eyes on me before!'

He did not realise that for kings, the world is very simple. Everyone is a subject.

'Come closer so I can see you better,' said the king, who was thrilled to be king over someone at last.

The little prince cast around for somewhere to sit, but

the planet was completely covered by the king's splendid ermine cloak. So he remained standing, but as he was tired, he started yawning.

'It is bad manners to yawn in the presence of a king,' said the monarch. 'I forbid it.'

'I can't help it,' replied the little prince, shamefaced. 'I've travelled a long way and I haven't slept.'

'Well then,' said the king, 'I command you to yawn. I haven't seen anyone yawn for years. Yawns are a curiosity for me. Go on, yawn again. That's an order.'

'Now I feel shy. I can't,' said the little prince, all flushed.

'Hmm! Hmm!' replied the king. 'Then I . . . I command you sometimes to yawn and sometimes to . . .'

He stammered a little and looked put out.

For what mattered to the king was to have his authority respected. He would not tolerate disobedience. He was an absolute monarch. But as he was also very kind, his orders were reasonable.

'If I commanded . . .' he would often say, '. . . if I commanded a general to turn into a sea bird, and the general disobeyed, it would not be the general's fault. It would be mine.'

'May I sit down?' timidly ventured the little prince.

'I command you to be seated,' replied the king, majestically gathering up a fold of his ermine cloak.

The little prince was amazed. The planet was minute. Over what could the king possibly reign?

'Your majesty,' he said, 'forgive me for asking you a question . . .'

'I command you to ask me a question,' said the king hastily.

'Your majesty . . . over what do you reign?'

'Over everything,' replied the king, with great simplicity.

'Over everything?'

With a broad sweep of his hand, the king indicated his planet, the other planets and the stars.

'Over all that?' queried the little prince.

'Over all that,' replied the king.

For not only was he an absolute monarch, he was also a universal monarch.

'And do the stars obey you?'

'Of course they do,' said the king. 'They obey instantly. I do not tolerate unruliness.'

Such power dazzled the little prince. Had he had that much power, he would have been able to watch not forty-four, but seventy-two, or a hundred, or even two hundred sunsets in one day, without having to move his chair! And, feeling a little homesick at the thought of his abandoned little planet, he made so bold as to ask the king a favour: 'I'd like to see a sunset. Please command the sun to go down . . . For me.'

'If I commanded a general to flit from one flower to

another like a butterfly, or to write a tragedy, or to turn into a sea bird, and if the general disobeyed my orders, who would be in the wrong, him or me?'

'It would be you,' said the little prince with certainty.

'Correct. One must only ask of a person what he can give,' the king went on. 'Authority is based principally on reason. If you command your people to go and throw themselves into the sea, they will revolt. I am entitled to demand obedience because my orders are reasonable.'

'What about my sunset?' the little prince reminded him. Once he had asked a question, he never let the matter drop.

'You'll have your sunset. I shall insist upon it. But in my wisdom, I shall wait until the conditions are favourable.'

'When will that be?' enquired the little prince.

'Ahem! Ahem!' replied the king, consulting a gigantic calendar. 'Ahem! Ahem! It will be around . . . around . . . it will be this evening around twenty minutes to eight! And you'll see how my commands are obeyed.'

The little prince yawned. He was disappointed to have missed his sunset. And besides, he was already feeling a little bored: 'There's nothing more for me to do here,' he said to the king. 'I'm going to set off on my travels again!'

'Don't go,' replied the king who was so proud to have a subject. 'Don't go, I'll make you a minister!'

'Minister of what?'

'Of . . . of justice!'

'But there's no one to judge!'

'You never know,' said the king. 'I haven't yet visited every corner of my kingdom. I am very old. There's no room for a carriage, and walking tires me.'

'Oh! But I've already seen it,' said the little prince leaning over to catch another glimpse of the far side of the planet. 'There's nobody over there either.'

'Then you will judge yourself,' replied the king. 'That's the hardest thing. It is much harder to judge oneself than to judge others. If you succeed in judging yourself well, then you are truly a wise man.'

'Well, I . . .' said the little prince, 'I can judge myself anywhere. I don't need to live here.'

'Ahem! Ahem!' said the king, 'I'm sure that there's an old rat somewhere. I hear him at night. You can judge that old rat. From time to time, you will sentence him to death. That way his life will depend on your decision. But you will pardon him each time so he is spared. There's only one rat.'

'Well, I . . .' replied the little prince, 'I don't like sentencing anyone to death so I think I'll definitely be off.'

'No,' said the king.

The little prince was ready to leave, but he did not want to offend the elderly monarch: 'If Your Majesty wishes to be obeyed on this occasion, he could give me a reasonable order. He could for example command me to leave before one minute is up. The conditions look favourable to me.'

The king did not reply. The little prince hesitated for a moment and then, with a sigh, he set off.

'I'm making you my ambassador,' the king shouted hastily after him.

He had an air of great authority.

Grown-ups really are very strange, mused the little prince as he continued on his travels.

Eleven

The second planet was inhabited by a show-off: 'Aha! Aha! A visit from an admirer!' cried the show-off from afar as soon as he spotted the little prince.

Show-offs imagine that everyone they meet must be an admirer.

'Hello,' said the little prince. 'You've got a funny hat.'

'It's for doffing when I bow,' replied the show-off.

'It's for doffing when people applaud me. Unfortunately, no one ever comes this way.'

'Really?' said the little prince, perplexed.

'Clap your hands,' the show-off instructed him. The little prince clapped his hands. The show-off bowed, modestly raising his hat.

This is much more fun than my visit to the king, thought the little prince. And he clapped his hands again. And once more the show-off began to bow and doff his hat.

After five minutes' clapping the little prince grew bored: 'And what must I do to make your hat fall off?' he asked.

But the show-off didn't hear him. Show-offs only hear praise.

'Do you really admire me a great deal?' he asked the little prince.

'What does "admire" mean?'

'Admire means recognising that I'm the smartest, handsomest, wealthiest and cleverest man on the planet.'

'But you're all alone on your planet!'

'Admire me anyway and make me a happy man!'

'I admire you,' said the little prince with a shrug. 'But why does it matter to you?'

And the little prince left.

Grown-ups really are very strange, mused the little prince as he continued on his travels.

Twelve

The next planet was inhabited by a drunkard. This visit was very short, but it deeply saddened the little prince.

'What are you doing?' he asked the drunkard, who was sitting silently in front of a collection of bottles, some empty and some full.

'I'm drinking,' replied the drunkard gloomily.

'Why do you drink?' the little prince asked.

'To forget,' replied the drunkard.

'To forget what?' enquired the little prince, who already felt sorry for him.

'To forget that I'm ashamed,' confessed the drunkard hanging his head.

'Ashamed of what?' asked the little prince, who wanted to help him.

'Ashamed of drinking!' ended the drunkard, withdrawing into a permanent silence.

And the little prince left, puzzled.

Grown-ups really are very strange, mused the little prince as he continued on his travels.

Thirteen

The fourth planet belonged to the businessman. This man was so absorbed that he did not even look up on the arrival of the little prince.

'Hello,' said the little prince. 'Your cigarette's gone out.'

'Three and two make five. Five and seven twelve. Twelve and three fifteen. Hello. Fifteen and seven twenty-two. Twenty-two and six twenty-eight. No time to re-light it. Twenty-six and five thirty-one. Phew! That makes five hundred and one million, six hundred and twenty-two thousand, seven hundred and thirty-one.'

'Five hundred million what?'

'Pardon? Are you still there? Five hundred million . . . I can't remember . . . I've got so much work! I'm a very busy man, no time to mess around! Two and five seven . . .'

'Five hundred and one million what?' repeated the little prince, who once he had asked a question, never let the matter drop.

The businessman glanced up: 'In all the fifty-four years I've lived on this planet, I have only been disturbed three times. The first time was twenty-two years ago, by a hornet that came from I-don't-know-where. It made a terrible racket and I made four mistakes in a sum. The second time was eleven years ago, by an attack of rheumatism – I don't get enough exercise. I don't have time to idle about either, I deal with serious matters. And the third time . . . is now! As I was saying five hundred and one million . . .'

'Million what?'

The businessman realised that there was no hope of peace: 'Million of those little things that you sometimes see in the sky.'

'Flies?'

'No, those little things that shine.'

'Bees?'

'No. Those little golden things that idlers day-dream about. But I don't have time to day-dream, I deal with serious matters!'

'Oh! Stars?'

'Yes, that's right. Stars.'

'And what will you do with five hundred million stars?'

'Five hundred and one million, six hundred and twenty-two thousand, seven hundred and thirty-one. I deal with serious matters, I am very precise.'

'And what do you do with these stars?'

'What do I do with them?'

'Yes.'

'Nothing. I own them.'

'You own the stars?'

'Yes.'

'But I've already met a king who . . .'

'Kings don't own. They "reign over". It's not the same thing at all.'

'And what's the use of your owning the stars?'

'It makes me rich.'

'And what's the use of being rich?'

'Then I can buy more stars, if anyone finds any.'

This man reasons a bit like the drunkard, thought the little prince.

And yet he carried on asking questions: 'How can you own the stars?'

'To whom do they belong?' retorted the businessman, grumpily.

'I don't know. To nobody.'

'Then they belong to me, because I thought of it first.'

'Is that enough?'

'Of course. When you find a diamond that doesn't belong to anyone, it's yours. When you find an island that doesn't belong to anyone, it's yours. When you are the first to have an idea, you patent it: it's yours. And I own the stars, because nobody ever thought of owning them before.'

'That's true,' said the little prince. 'And what do you do with them?'

'I manage them. I count and recount them,' said the businessman. 'It's a tough job but I work very hard!'

The little prince was still not satisfied.

'Well, if I have a scarf, I can wind it round my neck and wear it. If I have a flower, I can pick it and take it with me. But you can't pick the stars!'

'No, but I can put them in the bank.'

'What does that mean?'

'It means that I can write down on a piece of paper how many stars I own. And then I lock that piece of paper in a drawer.'

'And is that all?'

'It's enough!'

That's funny, thought the little prince. *It's rather poetic . . . not a serious business at all.*

When it came to serious matters, the little prince had very different ideas from grown- ups.

'Well,' he said, 'I have a flower that I water every day. I have three volcanoes that I chimney-sweep every week. Because I also sweep the one that's extinct. You never know. It's good for my volcanoes and it's good for my flower that I own them. But you're no good to the stars.'

The businessman opened his mouth, but couldn't think of anything to say, so the little prince left.

Grown-ups really are utterly extraordinary, he mused as he continued on his travels.

Fourteen

The fifth planet was very odd. It was the smallest of them all. There was just enough room for a lamp post and a lamplighter. The little prince simply could not understand the need for a lamp post and a lamplighter on a planet that had no houses and no people. Still, he reflected: 'This man may be absurd. But he's less absurd than the king, the show-off, the businessman or the drunkard. At least his job has a purpose. When he lights his lamp, it's as though he's creating another star, or a flower. When he puts out his lamp, he sends the flower or the star to sleep. It's a very nice job. It's really useful because it's nice.'

As he approached the planet he greeted the lamplighter politely: 'Hello. Why have you just put out your lamp?'

'Those are my orders,' replied the lamplighter. 'Hello.'

'What are your orders?'

'To put out my lamp. Good-night.' And he re-lit it.

'But why have you just re-lit it?'

'Those are my orders,' replied the lamplighter.

'I don't understand,' said the little prince.

'There's nothing to understand,' said the lamplighter. 'Orders are orders. Hello.'

And he put out his lamp.

Then he mopped his forehead with a red checked handkerchief.

'My job is terribly hard. It used to be simple. I'd put the lamp out in the morning and light it in the evening. I had the rest of the day to relax, and the rest of the night to sleep.'

'And have your orders changed?'

'My orders haven't changed,' said the lamplighter. 'And that's the problem! Each year the planet spins faster and faster but my orders haven't changed!'

'So?' said the little prince.

'So now the planet revolves once a minute, I don't have a moment's rest. I light the lamp and put it out once a minute!'

'That's funny! The days on your planet last a minute!'

'It's not funny at all,' said the lamplighter. 'We've already been chatting for a month.'

'A month?'

'Yes, thirty minutes. Thirty days! Good-night.' And he re-lit his lamp.

The little prince watched him and he liked this lamplighter who carried out his orders so faithfully. He thought of the sunsets on his own planet which he used to watch by simply moving his chair, and he wanted to help his friend: 'You know . . . I can think of a way you could rest when you wanted to . . .'

'I want to rest all the time,' said the lamplighter.

Strangely enough, a person can be both faithful to their job and lazy at the same time. The little prince went on: 'Your planet is so tiny that you can walk round it in three strides. All you need to do is walk slowly so you're always in the sun. When you want to rest, you walk . . . and the daylight will last as long as you want it to.'

'That doesn't help much,' said the lamplighter. 'What I like best is sleeping.'

'That's bad luck,' said the little prince.

'That is bad luck,' said the lamplighter. 'Hello.'

And he put out his lamp.

As the little prince continued on his journey, he reflected that all the others – the king, the show-off, the drunkard and the businessman – would look down on this man. *And yet he's the only person I don't find ridicu-*

lous. Maybe it's because he's looking after something other than himself.

He gave a sigh of regret and thought: *This man is the only one who could have been my friend. But his planet really is too small. There's no room for two.*

What the little prince did not dare admit to himself was that the main appeal of that particular planet was its fourteen hundred and forty sunsets every twenty-four hours!

Fifteen

The sixth planet was ten times bigger. It was inhabited by an elderly gentleman who wrote huge books.

'Well, well! An explorer!' he cried when he spotted the little prince.

The little prince perched on the table and got his breath back. He had already travelled such a long way!

'Where do you come from?' the elderly gentleman asked him.

'What's that big fat book?' said the little prince. 'What are you doing?'

'I'm a geographer,' said the elderly gentleman.

'What's a geographer?'

'A scholar who knows where the seas, rivers, towns, mountains and deserts are.'

'That's very interesting indeed,' said the little prince. 'Now that, at last, is a real job!' And he glanced about him at the geographer's planet. Never had he come across such a magnificent planet.

'Your planet's very beautiful. Are there any oceans?'

'I have no way of knowing,' said the geographer.

'Oh!' The little prince was disappointed.

'What about mountains?'

'I have no way of knowing,' said the geographer.

'What about cities and rivers and deserts?'

'I have no way of knowing that either,' said the geographer.

'But you're a geographer!'

'That is correct,' said the geographer, 'but I'm not an explorer. I'm desperately in need of explorers. It's not the geographer's job to count all the cities, rivers, mountains, seas, oceans and deserts. He is much too important to go strolling about. The geographer never leaves his desk. But the explorers come and see him. He questions them and notes down what they tell him. And if one of them tells him something interesting, the geographer has the explorer's character investigated.'

'Why?'

'Because an explorer who tells lies would be disastrous for the geography books. And so would an explorer who drinks too much.'

'Why?' asked the little prince.

'Because drunkards see double. So the geographer would note down two mountains when in fact there is only one.'

'I know someone who would be no good as an explorer,' said the little prince.

'That may be the case. So, when the explorer appears to be of good character, we investigate his discovery.'

'You go and see it?'

'No. That's too complicated. But we ask the explorer to provide evidence. For example, if he's discovered a big mountain, we ask him to bring us back big rocks.'

The geographer suddenly grew excited.

'But you come from a faraway place! You are an explorer! You are going to tell me about your planet!'

And so saying, the geographer opened his register and sharpened his pencil. Explorers' accounts are written in pencil at first. Once the explorer has provided evidence, they are written in ink.

'Well?' asked the geographer.

'Oh, my planet isn't of much interest,' said the little prince. 'It's tiny. I have three volcanoes. Two are active and one is extinct. But you never know.'

'You never know,' said the geographer.

'I also have a flower.'

'We don't record flowers,' said the geographer.

'Why not? They're the prettiest thing of all!'

'Because flowers are ephemeral.'

'What does "ephemeral" mean?'

'Geography books,' said the geographer, 'are the most important books of all. They never become outdated. It is very rare for a mountain to move. It is very rare for an ocean to dry up. We write down permanent facts.'

'But extinct volcanoes can wake up,' broke in the little prince. 'What does "ephemeral" mean?'

'Whether volcanoes are extinct or alive makes no difference to us,' said the geographer. 'What matters to us is the mountain. It doesn't change.'

'But what does "ephemeral" mean?' repeated the little prince, who once he had asked a question, never let the matter drop.

'It means "likely to die very soon".'

'Is my flower likely to die very soon?'

'Of course.'

My flower is ephemeral, thought little prince. *And she only has four thorns for protection! And I've left her all alone!*

That was his first pang of regret. But he perked up: 'What do you advise me to go and visit?' he asked.

'The planet Earth,' replied the geographer. 'We have good reports of it.'

And the little prince left, thinking about his flower.

Sixteen

A nd so the seventh planet was Earth.
Earth is not just any old planet. Altogether it has one hundred and eleven kings (including the African kings), seven thousand geographers, nine hundred thousand businessmen, seven and a half million drunkards and three hundred and eleven million show-offs. In other words around two billion grown-ups.

To give you an idea of the Earth's size, let me tell you for example that before electricity was invented, it was essential to maintain an army of four hundred and sixty-two thousand, five hundred and eleven lamplighters across all six continents.

Seen from a distance, the effect was magnificent. The movements of this army were choreographed like those of ballet dancers in an opera company. First it was the turn of the lamplighters of New Zealand and Australia. Then, having lit their lamps, they would go off to sleep. Next the lamplighters of China and Siberia joined the dance before they too withdrew to the wings. Then came the turn of the lamplighters of Russia and India, followed by those of Africa and Europe. Then those of South America. Then those of North America. And they never made a mistake in their order of appearance on stage. It was magnificent.

Only the lamplighter of the one lamp at the North Pole and his fellow lamplighter of the one lamp at the South Pole led carefree lives of idleness: they worked only twice a year.

Seventeen

Sometimes, when people want to sound clever, they make things up. I was not being completely truthful

when I told you about the lamplighters. I may have painted a false picture of our planet to those who do not know it. People actually take up very little space on Earth. If the Earth's two billion inhabitants were crammed together, they would easily fit into a public square twenty miles long and twenty miles wide. The whole human race could easily squeeze on to the tiniest Pacific island.

Grown-ups, of course, won't believe you.

They think they take up a lot more space. They think they are as big as baobabs. So then you tell them to do the sums. They love figures: they will like that. But do not waste time on this chore. There is no point. Trust me.

Once he had reached Earth, the little prince was very surprised not to see any people. He was already beginning to worry that he was on the wrong planet, when a moon-coloured coil wriggled in the sand.

'Good evening,' ventured the little prince on the off-chance.

'Good evening,' said the snake.

'What planet have I landed on?' asked the little prince.

'On Earth, in Africa,' replied the snake.

'Oh! . . . So aren't there any people on Earth?'

'This is the desert. There are no people in the deserts. Earth is very big,' said the snake.

The little prince sat down on a rock and gazed up at the sky: 'I wonder,' he said, 'whether the stars are lit up so that eventually each person will be able to find their own star. Look at my planet. It's just above us . . . but look how far away it is!'

'It's beautiful,' said the snake. 'What are you doing here?'

'I'm having a spot of bother with a flower,' said the little prince.

'Oh!' said the snake. And they fell silent.

'Where are all the people?' said the little prince at last. 'It's a bit lonely in the desert.'

'It's lonely among people too,' said the snake.

The little prince gazed at him pensively:

'You're a funny creature,' he said eventually, 'as slim as a finger . . .'

'But I am more powerful than the finger of a king,' said the snake.

The little prince smiled: 'You're not very powerful . . . you haven't even got feet . . . you can't even travel . . .'

'I can carry you farther than a ship,' said the snake. He wound himself around the little prince's foot, like a gold anklet: 'Those I touch, I return to the dust from whence they came,' he told him. 'But you are pure and you come from a star.'

The little prince did not reply.

'I feel sorry for you, you are so defenceless on this cruel Earth,' said the snake. 'If you feel homesick for your planet one day, I can help you. I can . . .'

'Oh! I understand perfectly well,' said the little prince. 'But why do you always speak in riddles?'

'I solve them all,' said the snake. And they fell silent.

Eighteen

The little prince crossed the desert and met only a plant. A plant with three petals, a tiny little flower.
'Hello,' said the little prince.
'Hello,' said the flower.

'Where are all the people?' the little prince enquired politely.

The flower had once seen a caravan go past: 'All the people? There are a few, I think, six or seven. I glimpsed them years ago. But you never know where to find them. The wind blows them about. They don't have roots, which causes them a lot of problems.'

'Goodbye,' said the little prince.

'Goodbye,' said the flower.

Nineteen

The little prince climbed to the peak of a high mountain. The only mountains he had ever seen were his three volcanoes and they only came up to his knees. And he used the extinct volcano as a stool. *From the top of a mountain as high as this,* he thought, *I'll be able to see the whole planet at once and all the people.* But he could see nothing except more jagged rocky peaks.

'Hello,' he said on the off-chance.

'Hello . . . Hello . . . Hello . . .' replied the echo.

'Who are you?' said the little prince.

'Who are you . . . who are you . . . who are you . . .' replied the echo.

'Be my friends, I'm all alone,' he said.

'All alone . . . All alone . . . All alone . . .' replied the echo.

What a funny planet! he thought. *It's all dry, and all pointed, and all salty. And the people have no imagination. They repeat everything you say . . . At home I had a flower: she always spoke first.*

Twenty

At last, having trudged for ages across sand, rocks and snow, the little prince came to a road. And all roads lead to people.

'Hello,' he said.

He was standing in front of a garden full of roses in bloom.

'Hello,' said the roses.

The little prince gazed at them. They all looked like his flower.

'Who are you?' he asked them in astonishment.

'We are roses,' said the roses.

'Oh!' said the little prince.

And he felt very unhappy. His flower had told him that she was the only one of her kind in the whole universe. And now, here were five thousand, all the same, in a single garden!

She'd be very upset if she saw this, he thought. *She'd cough a great deal and pretend to die to avoid looking stupid. And I would have to pretend to look after her, otherwise she'd actually allow herself to die, to spite me.*

Then, inwardly, he added: *I thought I was lucky to have one flower, but all I have is an ordinary rose. That and my three knee-high volcanoes, one of which is probably extinct. That doesn't make me much of a prince.* And he lay down in the grass and began to cry.

Twenty-One

That was when the fox appeared: 'Hello,' said the fox. 'Hello,' replied the little prince politely. He turned around but could not see anything.

'I'm over here,' said the voice. 'Under the apple tree.'

'Who are you?' said the little prince. 'You're very pretty.'

'I'm a fox,' said the fox.

'Come and play with me,' invited the little prince. 'I'm so sad.'

'I can't play with you,' said the fox. 'I'm not tame.'

'Oh! I'm sorry,' said the little prince. But on reflection, he asked: 'What does "tame" mean?'

'You're not from here,' said the fox. 'What are you looking for?'

'I'm looking for people,' said the little prince. 'What does "tame" mean?'

'People,' said the fox, 'have guns and they hunt. It's a real nuisance! They also breed chickens. That's all they're interested in. Are you looking for chickens?'

'No,' said the little prince. 'I'm looking for friends. What does "tame" mean?'

'It's something too readily forgotten,' said the fox. 'It means "creating a bond".'

'Creating a bond?'

'That's right,' said the fox. 'To me, you're just a little boy exactly like a hundred thousand other little boys. I don't need you, and you don't need me. To you, I'm a fox who's exactly like a hundred thousand other foxes. But, if you tame me, we will need each other. To me, you'll be absolutely unique, and to you, I'll be absolutely unique.'

'I'm beginning to see,' said the little prince.

'There's a flower . . . I think she tamed me.'

'It's possible,' said the fox. 'On Earth you see all manner of things.'

'Oh! It's not on Earth,' said the little prince.

The fox seemed greatly intrigued: 'On another planet?'

'Yes.

'Are there hunters on that planet?'

'No.'

'Very interesting! What about chickens?'

'No.'

'Nowhere's perfect,' sighed the fox.

And the fox went on: 'My life is boring. I hunt chickens, and men hunt me. All chickens are alike, and all men are alike. So I'm a little bored. But if you tame me, it will bring sunshine into my life. I'll be able to tell your footstep from all the others. The other footsteps drive me underground. Yours will draw me out of my lair, like music. And look! See the wheat fields over there? I don't eat bread. Wheat is no use to me. The wheat fields don't remind me of anything. And that's sad! But you have hair the colour of gold. So it will be wonderful when you've tamed me! The golden wheat will remind me of you. And the sound of the wind rustling the wheat will make me happy.'

The fox stopped talking and gazed at the little prince for a long time. 'Please, tame me!' he said.

'I'd love to,' replied the little prince, 'but I don't have much time. I've got friends to find and lots of things to understand.'

'You only understand the things you tame,' said the fox. 'People no longer have the time to understand anything. They buy things that are ready-made from the shops. But as there are no shops selling friends, people no longer have any friends. If you want a friend, tame me!'

'What do I have to do?' said the little prince.

'You must be very patient,' replied the fox. 'Sit down in the grass a little way away from me, like this. I'll watch you out of the corner of my eye and you won't say a word. Language is a source of misunderstanding. And each day, you can sit a little closer.'

The next day, the little prince returned.

'It would have been better if you'd come back at the same time,' said the fox. 'If you come at four o'clock in the afternoon, then from three o'clock I'll start feeling happy. The later it gets, the happier I'll feel. At four o'clock I'll already be getting agitated and worried; I'll discover the price of happiness! But if you come at any old time, I'll never know when to feel glad in my heart . . . we need rituals.'

'What's a ritual?' said the little prince.

'Something else that is too readily forgotten,' said the fox. 'It is what makes one day different from another, or one hour different from the other hours. My hunters have a ritual, for example. On Thursdays, they dance with the village girls. So Thursday is a wonderful day! I go for a stroll down to the vineyard. If the hunters danced any old time, all days would be alike, and I'd never have a day off.'

*

And so the little prince tamed the fox. And when the time came for him to leave: 'Oh!' said the fox, 'I'm going to cry.'

'It's your own fault,' said the little prince. 'I didn't mean to cause you any sorrow, but you wanted me to tame you.'

'That's right,' said the fox.

'But you're going to cry!' said the little prince.

'That's right,' said the fox.

'So you've gained nothing!'

'I have gained something – the colour of the wheat.'

Then he added: 'Go and see the roses again. You'll realise that yours is absolutely unique. Come back and say goodbye to me and I'll give you the gift of a secret.'

*

86

The little prince went off to see the roses again.

'You're not at all like my rose; you're nothing special yet,' he told them. 'Nobody has tamed you, and you haven't tamed anyone. My fox used to be like you. He was just a fox like a hundred thousand other foxes. But I made him my friend, and now he's absolutely unique.'

And the roses felt very uncomfortable.

'You are beautiful, but you are empty,' he added. 'Nobody would die for you. Of course, any ordinary person walking past *my* rose would think she was just like you. But she is much more important than all of you put together, because she's the one I watered. She's the one I sheltered under a glass dome, she's the one I protected with the screen. She's the one whose caterpillars I killed (except for the two or three for the butterflies). She's the one I listened to complaining, or boasting, or even sometimes being silent. Because she's *my* rose.'

*

And he went back to the fox: 'Goodbye,' he said.

'Goodbye,' said the fox. 'This is my secret. It's very simple. You only see clearly with your heart. The most important things are invisible to the eyes.'

'The most important things are invisible to the eyes,'

repeated the little prince, so that he would be sure to remember.

'It's the time you spent on your rose that makes your rose so important.'

'It's the time I spent on my rose . . .' said the little prince, so that he would be sure to remember.

'People have forgotten this simple truth,' said the fox. 'But you mustn't forget it. You are responsible for ever for those you have tamed. You are responsible for your rose.'

'I am responsible for my rose . . .' repeated the little prince, so that he would be sure to remember.

Twenty-Two

'Hello,' said the little prince.

'Hello,' said the signalman.

'So what do you do?' said the little prince.

'I sort the passengers into bundles of a thousand,' said the signalman. 'Sometimes I send the trains carrying them to the right, and sometimes to the left.'

And a lit-up express train, rumbling like thunder, made the signal box tremble.

'They're in a hurry,' said the little prince.

'What for?'

'The people in the train themselves don't know,' said the signalman.

And a second lit-up express train rumbled past in the opposite direction.

'Are they coming back already?' asked the little prince.

'They're not the same people,' said the signalman. 'It's an exchange.'

'Weren't they happy, where they were?'

'People are never happy where they are,' said the signalman.

And a third lit-up express train thundered past.

'Are they chasing the first passengers?' asked the little prince.

'They're not chasing anything at all,' said the signalman. 'They're sleeping in there, or they're yawning. Only the children press their noses against the windows.'

'Only children know what they're doing,' said the little prince. 'They'll play with a rag doll for hours, and that makes her very important to them, so if she's taken away from them, they cry.'

'They're lucky,' said the signalman.

Twenty-Three

'Hello,' said the little prince.
'Hello,' said the merchant.

He sold clever pills that can quench thirst.

You take one a week and you no longer feel the need to drink.

'Why do you sell those pills?' said the little prince.

'They save a lot of time,' said the merchant. 'The experts have done the sums. You save fifty-three minutes a week.'

'And what do you do with those fifty-three minutes?'

'You do whatever you like.'

'Well,' said the little prince, 'if I had fifty-three minutes to spare, I'd walk very slowly towards a drinking fountain.'

Twenty-Four

I had been marooned in the desert for a week, and the little prince had told me the story of the merchant as I drained the last drop of my water supply: 'Look here,' I said to the little prince, 'your stories are all very well, but I still haven't repaired my plane. I have nothing left to drink and I'd very much like to walk slowly towards a drinking fountain too!'

'My friend the fox . . .' he began.

'My little man, I don't want to hear any more about your fox!'

'Why not?'

'Because we're going to die of thirst.'

He could not follow my reasoning. He replied: 'It's good to have had a friend, even if you're going to die. Me, I'm very happy to have had a fox for a friend . . .'

He has no idea of the danger, I told myself. *He's never either hungry or thirsty. A little sunshine is all he needs.*

But he looked at me and answered my thought.

'I'm thirsty too. Let's go and look for a well.'

I gave a dismissive wave: it is absurd to go wandering around the vast desert in the hope of chancing upon a well. But we set off anyway.

After we had walked for hours, in silence, night fell and the stars began to shine. I saw them as if in a dream, as I had a slight fever from being so parched. The little prince's words danced in my memory.

'So are you thirsty too?' I asked him.

But he did not answer my question. He said simply: 'Water can be good for the heart, too.' I did not understand his reply, but I kept quiet. I knew better than to ask him questions. He was tired. He sat down. I sat down beside him.

After a silence, he said: 'The stars are beautiful, because of a flower we can't see.'

I replied, 'Of course,' and gazed in silence at the folds of the sand beneath the moon.

'The desert is beautiful,' he added.

And it was true. I have always loved the desert. You sit on a sand dune. You see nothing. You hear nothing. And yet something shines forth in the silence.

'What makes the desert more beautiful,' said the little prince, 'is that it's hiding a well somewhere.'

To my surprise, I suddenly understood the mysterious radiance concealed in the sands. When I was a little boy, I lived in an old house, and legend had it that there was treasure buried there. Of course, no one had ever been able to find it, or perhaps no one had ever even looked for it. But the hidden treasure enthralled the entire household. That house had a secret hidden deep in its heart.

'Yes,' I said to the little prince, 'whether it's a house, the stars or the desert, the thing that makes them beautiful is invisible!'

'I'm glad that you agree with my fox,' he said.

As the little prince was falling asleep, I gathered him up in my arms and set off again. I was moved. I felt as if I were carrying something delicate and precious. It even felt to me as if there were nothing more delicate on Earth. In the moonlight, I gazed at his pale forehead, closed eyes and locks of hair trembling in the wind, and thought: *What I see here is only his shell. The most important part is invisible.*

As his parted lips formed a half-smile, it struck me that what I found so deeply moving about the slumbering little prince was his loyalty to a flower; it was the image of a rose that burned in him like the flame of a lamp, even when he was asleep. And he felt even more delicate than before. You have to shield lamps well: a gust of wind can snuff them out.

And plodding on, at daybreak I discovered the well.

Twenty-Five

'People,' said the little prince, 'they dive into express trains, but they don't know what they're looking for. Then they get restless and go round in circles.'

And he added: 'It's not worth it.'

The well we had found was not like other Sahara wells. Sahara wells are simple holes dug in the sand. This one looked like a village well. But there was no village there and I thought I was dreaming.

'It's odd,' I said to the little prince, 'everything's there, the pulley, the bucket and the rope.'

He laughed, grabbed the rope and operated the pulley. It groaned like an old weather vane when the wind rises after being asleep for a long time.

'Listen,' said the little prince, 'we've roused the well and it's singing.'

I did not want him to get tired: 'Let me do that,' I said, 'it's too heavy for you.'

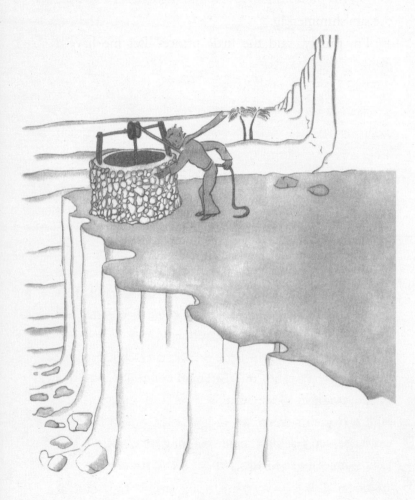

Slowly I hauled the bucket up to the rim of the well. I balanced it carefully. In my ears I could still hear the song of the pulley, and in the trembling water, I could see the sun shimmering.

'I'm thirsty,' said the little prince. 'Let me have a drink.'

And I understood what he had been looking for!

I raised the bucket to his lips. He drank, his eyes closed. It was the sweetest reward. This water was much more than mere nourishment. It was born from our journey under the stars, from the pulley's song, from my exertions. It was heart-warming, like a gift. When I was a little boy, the Christmas-tree lights, the music of midnight mass and the warmth of smiles were all part of the excitement of receiving a Christmas present.

'The people on your planet grow five thousand roses in one garden,' said the little prince, 'but they don't find what they are looking for there.'

'They don't find it,' I replied.

'And yet what they're looking for could be found in a single rose or in a little water.'

'Exactly,' I answered.

And the little prince added: 'But eyes are blind. You have to seek with the heart.'

I had drunk. I was breathing easily. The sand at

daybreak is the colour of honey. This honey colour too made me happy. So why did I feel heavy-hearted?

'You have to keep your promise,' whispered the little prince, who had sat down beside me once more.

'What promise?'

'You know, a muzzle for my little lamb. I am responsible for that flower!'

I took my rough drawings out of my pocket. The little prince flicked through them and said, laughing: 'Your baobabs look like cabbages.'

'Oh!' And I was so proud of my baobabs!

'Your fox . . . his ears . . . they're a bit like horns . . . and they're too long!' And he laughed again.

'You're being unfair, little man, I only knew how to draw an elephant inside a boa constrictor.'

'Oh! It'll be all right,' he said, 'children understand.'

So I sketched a muzzle. And I had a sense of foreboding as I gave it to him: 'You already have plans that I don't know about . . .'

But he did not reply. He said: 'You know, my fall to Earth . . . tomorrow's the anniversary . . .'

Then, after a silence, he added: 'I landed very close to this spot.'

And he reddened.

And again, without understanding why, I felt a strange sorrow. But there was one question that occurred to me: 'So it's no coincidence that, the morning I met you, a week ago, you were wandering around, all alone, miles and miles from anywhere! You were going back to the place where you had landed?'

The little prince turned red again.

And I added, hesitantly: 'Because, perhaps, of it being the anniversary?'

The little prince went red again. He never answered questions, but when people go red, that means yes, doesn't it?

'Oh!' I said. 'I'm afraid . . .'

But he replied: 'You have work to do now. You must go back to your machine. I'll wait here for you. Come back tomorrow night.'

But I was not reassured. I remembered the fox. Once you have allowed yourself to be tamed, you run the risk of feeling sadness . . .

Twenty-Six

Next to the well there was a crumbling ancient stone wall. The next night, when I came back from my work, I spotted my little prince from a distance, perched up on the wall, his legs swinging. And I could hear him talking: 'Don't you remember?' he was saying. 'It's not here exactly!'

Someone no doubt replied, because I heard the little prince argue: 'Yes it was! Yes it was! It's the right day, but this is not the right place.' I continued walking towards the wall. I could still neither hear nor see anybody. But again the little prince was speaking: '... Of course. You'll see where my footprints begin in the sand. All you need to do is wait. I'll be there tonight.'

I was twenty metres from the wall and still I could not see anything.

The little prince said again, after a silence: 'Is your venom potent? You're sure you won't make me suffer for long?'

I came to a halt, my heart full of dread, but still I did not understand.

'Now go away,' he said, 'I want to get down!'

Then I glanced down to the foot of the wall and I gave a start. There, rearing towards the little prince, was one of those yellow snakes that kill you in thirty seconds. Fumbling in my pocket for my pistol, I raced over, but at the noise I made, the snake gently slithered away, like a

stream of water sinking into the sand, and languidly threaded its way between the rocks with a soft rasping sound. I reached the wall just in time to catch my little prince, pale as snow.

'What on earth are you up to! Do you talk with snakes now!'

I unwound the gold scarf he always wore. I moistened his temples and gave him a drink of water. And now I did not dare ask him anything more. He gazed at me solemnly and put his arms around my neck. I could feel his heart fluttering like that of a dying bird that has been shot. He said to me: 'I'm glad you've found what you needed for your machine. You'll be able to go home now . . .'

'How do you know!'

That was exactly what I had come to tell him – that, against all the odds, I had managed to repair my plane!

He did not answer my question, but added: 'Me too, today, I'm going home.'

Then wistfully: 'It's much farther . . . it's much harder.'

I was aware that something extraordinary was happening. I hugged him like a little child, but yet he seemed to be sliding vertically into an abyss and there was nothing I could do to hold him back.

His expression was solemn, his gaze vacant: 'I've got

your lamb. And I've got the crate for the lamb. And I've got the muzzle.'

And he smiled sadly.

I waited a long time. I could feel him gradually growing warmer: 'Little man, you were afraid.'

He had been afraid, of course! But he laughed softly: 'I'll be a lot more afraid tonight.'

Once again I shivered with a sense of the inevitable. And I realised that I could not bear the idea of never hearing that laugh again. To me it was like a tinkling spring in the desert.

'Little man, I want to hear you laugh again.'

But he said: 'Tonight it will be one year. My star will be just above the spot where I fell last year.'

'Little man, tell me this business with a snake and a star is just a bad dream.'

But he did not reply. He simply said: 'The things that matter are invisible.'

'Yes, they are.'

'It's like with the flower. If you love a flower who happens to be on a star, you love to watch the sky at night. All the stars have flowers.'

'Yes, they do.'

'It's like with the water. The water you gave me to drink was like music, because of the pulley and the rope . . . you remember . . . it was good.'

'Yes, it was.'

'You'll watch the stars at night. My planet's too small for me to point it out to you. It's better that way. My star will be just another star in the sky. That way you'll love watching all the stars. They will all be your friends. Besides, I'm going to give you a present.'

He laughed again.

'Oh! Little man, I love hearing you laugh!'

'And that's exactly what my present will be . . . it will be like it was with the water . . .'

'What do you mean?'

'People have stars but they're not all the same. For those who travel, the stars are guides. For others, they are nothing but little lights. For others, who are scientists, they are problems. For my businessman, they were gold. Those stars are all silent. But you will have stars that are completely different . . .'

'What do you mean?'

'When you look at the sky at night, because I'll be living on one of them, because I'll be laughing on one of them, to you it will sound as if all the stars are laughing. You will have stars that can laugh!'

And he laughed again.

'And when you have found consolation – as people always do – you will be glad to have known me. You will always be my friend. You'll want to laugh with me. And sometimes you will open your window, just like that, for the pleasure . . . and your friends will be astonished to see you looking at the sky and laughing. Then you'll say to them: "Yes, the stars always make me laugh!" and they'll think you're mad. What a mischievous trick I'll have played on you.'

And he laughed again.

'It will be as if, instead of stars, I'd given you lots of little laughing bells.'

And he laughed again. Then he became solemn: 'Tonight . . . you know . . . don't come.'

'I shan't leave you.'

'I'll look as if I'm in pain . . . I'll look as if I'm dying. That's the way it is. Don't come and see that, it's not worth it.'

'I shan't abandon you.' But he was concerned.

'I'm saying that . . . it's also because of the snake. It mustn't bite you . . . snakes are evil. They can bite for the fun of it.'

'I shan't abandon you.'

Then he added, reassured: 'Luckily they have no venom left for a second bite.'

That night he slipped away soundlessly, and I didn't see him leave. When I managed to catch up with him, he was walking purposefully, with rapid strides. Suddenly, he said to me: 'Oh! You're here.'

And he took my hand. But he was still fretting: 'You shouldn't have come. You will be upset. I'll look as if I'm dead, but I won't be.'

I said nothing.

'It's too far, you understand. I can't carry this body. It's too heavy.'

I said nothing.

'But it will be like an old skin that has been shed. Old skins aren't sad.'

I said nothing.

He became a little dispirited, but he made one more effort: 'It'll be nice, you know. I'll watch the stars too. All the stars will be wells with a rusty pulley. All the stars will pour me water to drink.'

I said nothing.

'It'll be so wonderful! You'll have five hundred million bells, and I'll have five hundred million wells.'

And he fell silent too, because he was crying.

*

'We're here. Let me take a step on my own.'

And he sat down because he was afraid.

Then he said: 'You know ... my flower ... I'm responsible for her! And she's so fragile! She's so innocent. And she only has four tiny thorns for protection.'

And I sat down because my legs would no longer hold me up. He said: 'There ... That's all ...'

He hesitated a little longer, then he stood up again. He took a step forward. But I was rooted to the spot.

There was a yellow flash in the region of his ankle. He remained motionless for an instant.

He didn't cry out. He fell softly, the way a tree falls. He didn't even make a thud, because of the sand.

Twenty-Seven

And now, six years have passed already. I have never told anyone this story. My friends were very happy to see me alive. I was sad, but I told them: 'It's exhaustion.'

Now, I have found some consolation, although I am still sad. But I know that the little prince made it back to his planet, because, at daybreak, I saw that his body was not there. It was not a very heavy body . . . And at night, I love listening to the stars. It is like hearing five hundred million bells.

But here is an extraordinary thing: on the muzzle that I drew for the little prince I forgot the leather strap! He will never have been able to put it on the lamb. So I wonder what happened on his planet. Maybe the lamb ate the flower.

Sometimes I think: Surely not! The little prince places the glass dome over his flower every night to protect her, and he keeps a close eye on his lamb. So I am happy, and all the stars laugh softly.

At other times I say to myself: A person can get distracted and that's it! One night he forgot the glass dome, or the lamb slipped away unnoticed. Then the bells all turn to tears!

*

And it is all a huge mystery. For those of you who love the little prince as I do, nothing in the universe looks the same, depending on whether, somewhere out there, a little lamb has or has not eaten a rose.

Look at the sky. Ask yourself: 'Has the lamb eaten the flower, yes or no?' And you will see how everything is different.

And no grown-up will ever understand how important that is!

This, for me, is the most beautiful and the saddest landscape in the world. It is the same landscape as on the previous page, but I have drawn it again to show you. It is here that the little prince appeared on Earth, and then disappeared.

Look carefully at this landscape so as to be certain to recognise it if you travel to the African desert one day. And, if you happen to pass by this place, I urge you not to hurry, but to wait a little under the star. If you come across a golden-haired child who laughs and never answers your questions, you will know who he is. So, please, write and comfort me by telling me he has come back.

PICADOR CLASSIC

On 6 October 1972, Picador published its first list of eight paperbacks. It was a list that demonstrated ambition as well as cultural breadth, and included great writing from Latin America (Jorge Luis Borges's *A Personal Anthology*), Europe (Hermann Hesse's *Rosshalde*), America (Richard Brautigan's *Trout Fishing in America*) and Britain (Angela Carter's *Heroes and Villains*). Within a few years, Picador had established itself as one of the pre-eminent publishers of contemporary fiction, non-fiction and poetry.

What defines Picador is the unique nature of each of its authors' voices. The Picador Classic series highlights some of those great voices and brings neglected classics back into print. New introductions – personal recommendations if you will – from writers and public figures illuminate these works, as well as putting them into a wider context. Many of the Picador Classic editions also include afterwords from their authors which provide insight into the background to their original publication, and how that author identifies with their work years on.

Printed on high quality paper stock and with thick cover boards, the Picador Classic series is also a celebration of the physical book.

Whether fiction, journalism, memoir or poetry, Picador Classic represents timeless quality and extraordinary writing from some of the world's greatest voices.

Discover the history of the Picador Classic series and
the stories behind the books themselves at
www.picador.com/classic